Louder, Lili

Gennifer Choldenko

illustrated by

S. D. Schindler

G. P. PUTNAM'S SONS

G. P. PUTNAM'S SONS
A division of Penguin Young Readers Group.
Published by The Penguin Group.
Penguin Group (USA) Inc., 375 Hudson Street, New York, NY 10014, U.S.A.
Penguin Group (Canada), 90 Eglinton Avenue East, Suite 700, Toronto, Ontario,
Canada M4P 2Y3 (a division of Pearson Penguin Canada Inc.).
Penguin Books Ltd, 80 Strand, London WC2R ORL, England.
Penguin Ireland, 25 St. Stephen's Green, Dublin 2, Ireland (a division of Penguin Books Ltd.).
Penguin Group (Australia), 250 Camberwell Road, Camberwell, Victoria 3124, Australia
(a division of Pearson Australia Group Pty Ltd).
Penguin Books India Pvt Ltd, 11 Community Centre, Panchsheel Park, New Delhi - 110 017, India.
Penguin Group (NZ), 67 Apollo Drive, Mairangi Bay, Auckland 1311, New Zealand
(a division of Pearson New Zealand Ltd.)
Penguin Books (South Africa) (Pty) Ltd, 24 Sturdee Avenue, Rosebank,
Johannesburg 2196, South Africa.
Penguin Books Ltd, Registered Offices: 80 Strand, London WC2R ORL, England.

Published simultaneously in Canada. Manufactured in China by South China Printing Co. Ltd.
Design by Gina DiMassi. Text set in Humana Sans Bold.
Library of Congress Cataloging-in-Publication Data available on request.

ISBN 978-0-399-24252-6
1 3 5 7 9 10 8 6 4 2
First Impression

To Ian and Kai
—G. C.

To Forest Park Elementary School
—S. D. S.

When Lili heard her name, she answered "here" in a voice so soft, you couldn't hear it even if you wanted to.

Mrs. Backmeyer marked Lili absent.

When Lili heard "All right, everyone, find a partner,"
Lili's stomach twisted and her mouth froze closed.

Every kid had a partner . . . except Lili.

"You with the ponytail. Come be my partner,"
Mrs. Backmeyer said. The whole class stared at Lili.

"Lili, sweetheart, you have to learn to speak up," Mrs. Backmeyer said, erasing the zero by Lili's name.

Mrs. Backmeyer did not have a speaking-up problem. Her voice was so loud, you had to listen to it whether you wanted to or not. Even the birds in the sky and the fishes in the sea heard Mrs. Backmeyer, and they all did what she said.

At recess Lili did not go out
to play. She curled up in a corner
of the classroom next to Lois,
the guinea pig, and read books.
Only Lois knew she was there.

After recess Mrs. Backmeyer asked who wanted to take care of Lois. Arms shot up around Lili. Wild arms. Waving arms. Arms that flew in all directions.

Lili wanted to raise her hand. But her hand would not go up.

Rita B. got to take care of Lois. Rita B. got to take her out of her cage. Rita B. got to fill her water and pour the seeds into her dish.

"How was school today?" Lili's mom asked when she
picked Lili up. "Did you have someone to eat lunch with?"

"Lois," Lili said.

"That's nice," her mom said. "What's her last name?
I'll invite her whole family over for dinner."

"She's an orphan," Lili said.

"Oh, dear, you be nice to her, Lili Ann."

The next day, when it was time to find partners, a girl named Cassidy grabbed Lili's arm. "You're my partner for rhyming pond," Cassidy announced. "You write the rhymes. I'll color the fishies."

"*Squishy, fishy. Itchy, witchy. Cookie dough, Oreo.* Who did these?" Mrs. Backmeyer asked. "They're terrific!"
"I did," Cassidy said.

During lunch, Cassidy wanted to share. "You get the carrots.
I get the cake," she said.

In science, Cassidy got the butterflies, Lili got the dirt.
And in reading corner, Cassidy got *Secrets of Fairy World* and
Lili got *The Big Book of Grammar Rules*.

Every day after that, Cassidy picked Lili as a partner.
"Lili is my best friend," Cassidy said.

But Lili stood with Lois, watching Rita B. clean her cage.

Then one day Mrs. Backmeyer got laryngitis.
Mrs. Snyderman was there. Mrs. Snyderman didn't do
partners. Mrs. Snyderman didn't do much of anything,
except talk on her cell to Mr. Snyderman.

"Hey," said Cassidy, "let's take Lois out."
Cassidy opened the cage and picked up Lois.
"May I have a turn?" asked Lili in a voice you
didn't have to hear if you didn't want to.
Cassidy didn't want to.

"Let's give Lois a haircut,"
said Cassidy, grabbing the
scissors.

"Hey! Don't do that,"
said Lili.

"I'm going to tell,"
said Rita B.

"Who are you going to tell?"
Cassidy asked. "Mrs. Spiderman?"

Mrs. Snyderman was in the bathroom. She'd been in there a long time—
much longer than it took to do your business no matter what kind it was.

"Leave Lois alone," said Lili in the loudest voice she had ever used in her whole entire life . . . but Cassidy didn't hear.

"Let's pour glue in her water," Cassidy said.

Lili wished Mrs. Backmeyer was there with all her might. But Mrs. Backmeyer wasn't there. No teacher was there.

Cassidy grabbed Lois's water bottle. She tipped the glue forward.

Lili's face burned. Her mouth tasted like Tabasco sauce. From deep inside came a voice so loud, it made the windows rattle, the desks rumble and the rug come up off the floor.

"STOP IT!"

Everyone stopped it. The kids in Lili's class. The kids in the classroom next door. The birds in the sky and the fishes in the sea—they all stopped it too. Even the glue in the bottle stood still.

"Give her here!" Lili said.
"You coulda just told me you wanted a turn.
You didn't have to get all bossy," Cassidy said.

"Let's put her back in the cage," said Rita B.
"We won't let Cassidy near her," said Lili.
"Ever again," said Rita B.

When Mrs. Backmeyer came back to school, she still couldn't speak very loudly. "Pick partners," she whispered.

"Rita B.?" Lili asked in a voice just loud enough for Rita to hear.

"Lili," said Rita B., taking her hand.